A Note to Parents

Eyewitness Readers is a compelling new program for beginning readers, designed in conjunction with leading literacy experts, including Dr. Linda Gambrell, President of the National Reading Conference and past board member of the International Reading Association.

Eyewitness has become the most trusted name in illustrated books, and this new series combines the highly visual *Eyewitness* approach with engaging, easy-to-read stories. Each *Eyewitness Reader* is guaranteed to capture a child's interest while developing his or her reading skills, general knowledge, and love of reading.

The four levels of *Eyewitness Readers* are aimed at different reading abilities, enabling you to choose the books that are exactly right for your children:

Level One – Beginning to read
Level Two – Beginning to read alone
Level Three – Reading alone
Level Four – Proficient readers

The "normal" age at which a child begins to read can be anywhere from three to eight years old, so these levels are intended only as a general guideline.

No matter which level you select, you can be sure that you are helping your child learn to read, then read to learn!

J
597.8
W191
JP

A DK PUBLISHING BOOK
www.dk.com

Project Editors Caroline Bingham
and Penny Smith
Designer Michelle Baxter
Senior Editor Linda Esposito
Managing Art Editor Peter Bailey
US Editor Regina Kahney
Production Josie Alabaster
Editorial Consultant
Theresa Greenaway

Reading Consultant
Linda B. Gambrell, Ph.D.

First American Edition, 1998
2 4 6 8 10 9 7 5 3
Published in the United States by
DK Publishing, Inc.
95 Madison Avenue, New York, New York 10016

Published in Great Britain by Dorling Kindersley Limited.

Library of Congress Cataloging-in-Publication Data
Wallace, Karen.
    Tale of a tadpole / by Karen Wallace. -- 1st American ed.
    p.   cm. -- (Eyewitness readers. Level 1)
    Summary: Describes the development of a tadpole.
    ISBN 0-7894-3437-7 (pbk.) --
    ISBN 0-7894-3761-9 (hc : alk. paper).
    1. Tadpoles--Juvenile literature. [1. Tadpoles.] I. Title. II. Series.
QL668.E2W264 1998
597.8'139--dc21
                                            98-14976
                                               CIP
                                               AC

Color reproduction by Colourscan, Singapore
Printed and bound in Belgium by Proost

Photography by Paul Bricknell, Jane Burton, Geoff Dann,
Mike Dunning, Neil Fletcher, Frank Greenaway, Kim Taylor

EYEWITNESS READERS

BEGINNING
1
TO READ

Tale of
a Tadpole

Written by Karen Wallace

DK PUBLISHING, INC.

The tale of a tadpole
begins in a pond.
Mother frog lays her eggs
next to a lily pad.

Each tiny egg
is wrapped
in clear jelly.

jelly

5

Inside the jelly
the eggs grow into tadpoles.
They wriggle like worms.

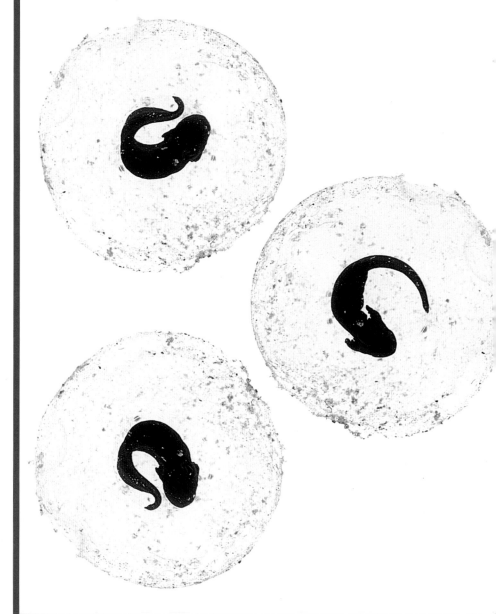

They push through the jelly
and swim in the water.

They breathe through gills,
just like fishes.

gills

Many other animals
live in the pond.

Shiny goldfish
and sticklebacks.
And great diving beetles.

They chase the young tadpoles.

A stickleback feels hungry.
He opens his mouth wide.

The little gray tadpoles
wriggle their tails ...

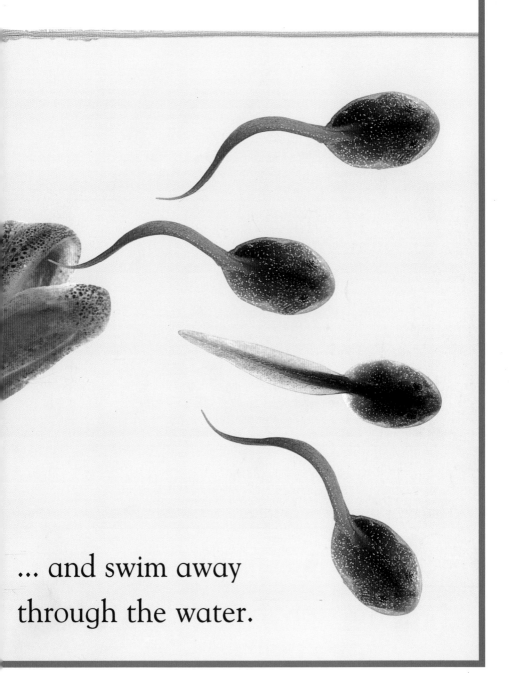

... and swim away
through the water.

A great diving beetle
feels hungry too.

His hairy back legs
beat through the water.

The tadpoles escape
and hide in the weeds.

Soon a tadpole
grows legs
with tiny webbed toes.

webbed
toes

Webbed toes are like flippers.
They help the small tadpole
push through the water.

He grows arms
with long skinny fingers.

fingers

He nibbles on plants and
gobbles green pondweed.

Half tadpole, half frog,
he rests in the sunshine.

His tail is shrinking.

tail

It gets smaller and smaller.

The new little frog
sits on a lily pad.

His legs are strong now.
He can breathe through his nostrils.
His skin is dotted
with tiny gold spots.

nostril

Frogs must keep their skin slimy.
He hops back in the pond
and swims for a while.
Then he climbs onto a log.

Another frog climbs up
and sits down beside him.

Now full-grown,
he dives through the water.

He's not afraid of the stickleback.
He swims past the beetle.

In the pond
he watches and waits.
What does he see
with his round beady eye?

eye

A fly lands
above him.
He creeps
closer and closer.

But a big frog jumps up.
It snatches the fly
with its long, sticky tongue.

tongue

The frog
misses his meal.
Next time
he'll be faster!

The golden-skinned frog
chases a dragonfly.
It lands on a lily pad.
Under the lily pad are
hundreds of frogs' eggs.

Inside each egg
a tadpole is growing.
Each tadpole will grow
into a golden-skinned frog.

Picture Word List

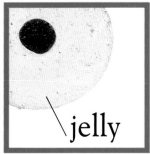

jelly

page 5

tail

page 18

gills

page 7

nostril

page 21

webbed toes

page 14

eye

page 26

fingers

page 16

tongue

page 28

▣ EYEWITNESS READERS

Level 1 *Beginning to Read*

A Day at Greenhill Farm
Truck Trouble
Tale of a Tadpole
Surprise Puppy!
Duckling Days
A Day at Seagull Beach
Whatever the Weather
Busy, Buzzy Bee

Level 2 *Beginning to Read Alone*

Dinosaur Dinners
Fire Fighter!
Bugs! Bugs! Bugs!
Slinky, Scaly Snakes!
Animal Hospital
The Little Ballerina
Munching, Crunching, Sniffing, and Snooping
The Secret Life of Trees

Level 3 *Reading Alone*

Spacebusters
Beastly Tales
Shark Attack!
Titanic
Invaders from Outer Space
Movie Magic
Plants Bite Back!
Time Traveler

Level 4 *Proficient Readers*

Days of the Knights
Volcanoes
Secrets of the Mummies
Pirates!
Horse Heroes
Trojan Horse
Micromonsters
Going for Gold!